T0284168

The Secret Diary of
Chumleigh the Cat

Transcribed by
Paul Lawrence

Illustrated by
Nicki Averill

tfm publishing Ltd, Castle Hill Barns, Harley, Nr Shrewsbury, SY5 6LX, UK
Tel: +44 (0)1952 510061; Fax: +44 (0)1952 510192
E-mail: info@tfmpublishing.com; Web site: www.tfmpublishing.com

Editing: Nikki Bramhill BSc (Hons) Dip Law
Illustrations: Nicki Averill Design & Illustration, www.nickiaverilldesign.co.uk
Design & Typesetting: Nicki Averill

Hardback	ISBN: 978-1-913755-28-7
E-book editions:	© 2024
ePub	ISBN: 978-1-913755-29-4
Mobi	ISBN: 978-1-913755-30-0
Web pdf	ISBN: 978-1-913755-31-7

Printed by Gutenberg Press Ltd., Gudja Road, Tarxien, GXQ 2902, Malta
Tel: +356 2398 2201; Fax: +356 2398 2290; Web site: www.gutenberg.com.mt

Special thanks to Freckle and Scribble who have been inspirational for the illustrations.

Introduction

We have lived with cats for long enough to come to realise that they are independent, strong-minded creatures.

Cats are not like other pets. No one owns a cat like they do a dog, a hamster or a guinea pig. Cats live by their own rules. It has been said that dogs have owners and cats have staff.

In writing this book, I've rather let my imagination run riot by looking at life through the eyes of a cat. I've tried to interpret what cats are thinking about life and their surroundings and have endeavoured to add a modicum of humour.

Over the years our cats have been Sam, a ginger tom, Merlin, a most naughty black and white male, Molly, a gentle long-haired female and Patches, a loving but belligerent tortoiseshell female. There is a little of all of them in this book and I treasure their memories. However, any resemblance to any human beings, alive or otherwise, is purely coincidental.

Of course, there is also a little of me in this book and close friends may recognise some of my pet subjects within the text.

I hope it brings you a chuckle or two and that any cat owners out there will pause for a moment now and again and ponder what their cat is really thinking!

Paul Lawrence
Shropshire, UK
June 2024

JANUARY 1

Dear diary,

Apparently, it is the first day of a brand new year; I can barely contain my excitement.

The humans were late getting up and I'm not surprised based on the noise they made coming in last night. She fell over twice getting up the stairs and he is going to be in so much trouble when she wakes up and realises that he pissed in the wardrobe, by mistake I trust, before collapsing into bed.

I've had to wait so long this morning for my breakfast that I thought I was going to faint. I think it is going to be a quiet day in the house today after some early shouting.

JANUARY 2

Dear diary,

Well, I suppose I should have a token stab at making some New Year resolutions.

The norm in this house is that they don't last beyond the end of January and crash and burn a lot sooner than that in many cases. Anyway, here are mine. I've given them considerable thought and feel that they will be both attainable and make the world (well, my world) a better place. As Ant and Dec would say, in no particular order, they are to get the best food, find the cosiest places to snooze, irritate dogs whenever possible, get revenge on people who are nasty to me and avoid going to the vets.

Simples.

JANUARY 11

Dear diary,

What buffoon invented Tuesday? It's not the start of the week; it's not the middle of the week. Treats provisioned for the weekend have been consumed and it's the day she usually washes the kitchen floor.

As far as I can see, nothing good will ever come of Tuesday.

I think I shall spend this one sleeping and hope it will all soon be over.

JANUARY 16

Dear diary,

You would
not believe
the lengths
I had to go to
this morning just to
get my breakfast. Okay, I
know it was a Sunday, but come
on! I even waited until it got light before
I started the strategies that usually work. I made it easy for starters:
I jumped on the bed and gently rubbed my head against hers.
Nothing. I sat on top of her and started kneading the bed clothes
with my paws. Even when I got the claws out, all I got was a rude
grunt and a push to get off the bed. Next, I tried wailing loudly
and mournfully with frustration, which usually gets a response.
This time she put the pillow over her head. Things were now
getting desperate so I pulled out the big guns and started climbing
up the curtains. That did it and she finally got out of bed. Clearly,
she was not amused and I got sworn at all the way to the fridge.
If only she'd got out of bed when I first asked, we could have
avoided all that unpleasantness! I really don't understand humans.

JANUARY 20

Dear diary,

I really have nothing to report today. It is a nothing day filled with nothingness.

I'll probably go back to sleep and dream of days filled with action, drama and tuna.

JANUARY 22

Dear diary,

How was I to know it wasn't for me?

She placed a nice warm roast chicken on the kitchen table and then left the room when the phone rang. It was probably her friend Beryl who can flap her gums to an Olympic standard. Anyway, while they were yabbering away about nothing, I couldn't resist the smell of freshly roasted chicken, so I hopped up onto a chair and then the table. I sort of knew this was wrong, but I thought I'd just nibble a tiny morsel and then leave.

No one would ever know, would they?

What could possibly go wrong?

But I got hold of a rather bigger bite than I'd planned and very quickly it all started to go terribly wrong. As I tugged at the chicken, I moved backwards but rather unluckily lost my footing as I went off the edge of the table. Unfortunately, I took the chicken with me and I was very lucky to avoid serious injury as this substantial chicken, which had clearly forgotten how to fly whilst in the oven, and its cooking tray plummeted to the floor. I just had to leg it and let the heat die down for a few hours.

At least it got her off the phone to Beryl!

How was I to know it wasn't for me?

JANUARY 30

Dear diary,

Oh, dear God, there's snow on the ground.

I had to go out just now to answer a call of
nature and my paws are freezing. If anyone
wants me, I will be in the airing cupboard
for the rest of the day. Only disturb me
if you are bringing food or my life is in
mortal danger.

FEBRUARY 2

Dear diary,

I've tried so hard to be good today. I waited patiently to be served my breakfast, found somewhere acceptable to sleep, didn't kill anything and greeted them warmly when they came home from work. But still I got into trouble. I knew the wheel was about to come off when she went into the lounge and said to him: "Can you smell that?" Unfortunately, I had been rumbled. In the small hours of the night, I'd inadvertently barfed up the remains of a mouse behind the sofa and I'd fervently hoped that the smell would have dissipated by the time they headed to the lounge to turn the tellybox on. Yet again, I am in trouble and not feeling very loved. I think the mouse must have been off.

FEBRUARY 7

Dear diary,

I hate it when it rains all day as it really interferes with my toilet habits. Usually, I'll pop outside a couple of times during the day to answer the call of nature, but when it is chucking it down I really don't want to go out. I hate getting my fur wet. So, today, I decided conditions were just too bad. Instead, I used the mat inside the front door to do what a cat needs to do. I thought the humans would spot the offending 'Richard the third' and put it outside with minimal fuss. What I didn't expect was for her to come bursting through the door, wrestling with an umbrella and briskly wiping her wet shoes on the door mat without even glancing down first. Oh dear, what a mess…

FEBRUARY 10

Dear diary,

I think one of our neighbours is a snowflake. He's constantly wittering on about how terrible things are and he seems to be offended by his own shadow. He's taken to starting petitions on all the things that offend him and it is a steadily growing list.

He keeps knocking on the door looking for signatures to support his latest crusade. In the last month or two he's been offended by the colour of paint used on the house at the end of the road, the early morning whistling of the bin men, the skanky old truck parked on the drive at one of his neighbour's houses and the union jack flag on the flag pole in the garden at number 23.

I think he should just grow a pair and put up with it. I'd like to grow a pair to replace the ones confiscated by the vet when I was a youngster.

FEBRUARY 16

Dear diary,

To be honest, I do wonder why I bother keeping humans.
If I could operate a tin opener, I'd really have no need for them.

If I look at the pros and cons of the deal, they come out way
ahead. I get food served, often at random times when they can
be bothered rather than when I want it. However, they get the
endless enjoyment of having a cat in their house; someone to talk
at when they are bored/lonely/cross/upset/frustrated, someone to
make a fuss of when it suits them and
someone in the house when they
get home from what they
usually claim has been
another tough day at the
office. And all I get in
return is tins opened.

It really is most
inequitable.

FEBRUARY 23

Dear diary,

Well, I'm a little recovered today. Yesterday they took me to the vets, or the torture dungeon as I call it.

It was a ghastly experience and I've only just stopped shaking enough to start recording my thoughts. It was such a traumatising experience that I can only relate the full horror story in several diary entries. It all began when the pet carrier, or the lunar module as I call it, was fetched from the basement. This was a very ominous sign and I hid away as best I could. But they found me and wrestled me towards the lunar module. I tried my best trick for not going in, which I call the starfish move. I put all four legs out as far as I could and tried to lock them in the straight position. This makes it very difficult to put me inside, but I was overcome by a greater power.

To be continued…

FEBRUARY 24

Dear diary,

I left you as I was being forced into the lunar module. Next, I was helpless as they put me into the car or the conveyance of doom as I call it. Although in fact it is a 57-plate Ford Mondeo with a dodgy gearbox and broken air-con. I knew this could only mean one thing: I was being taken to the vets. How I didn't soil myself on the 10-minute journey, I'll never know. Once parked, we entered the reception of doom and they cheerily reported that I was here for my annual flu jab, worming and flea treatment.

Oh, the shame.

By the way, no one checked with me to see if this appointment fitted my busy schedule. That would have been nice. To be continued again…

FEBRUARY 25

Dear diary,

In the waiting room at the Hammer House of Horror, they made all the usual silly noises at me through the bars of my cage. The odd finger got poked through the bars in some half-arsed attempt to make me feel better about the situation. It failed. I did not wish to be there, incarcerated.

I strongly considered sinking my teeth into one of the offending fingers to show my true feelings. That would have shown them. Instead, I gulped loudly when I heard my name called out and I'm pretty sure that a bit of wee came out.

To be continued…

FEBRUARY 26

Dear diary,

As suspected, it got worse when I was taken into the inner torture chamber where the chief torturer was waiting. He looked about 14 and I was desperate for someone to ask if he was really old enough to be doing this. But before I could attempt to show my concerns, he came at me with a thermometer and, after what seemed like a pretty fair run-up, he shoved it straight up where the sun doesn't shine. I was completely taken aback and tried to adequately express my discomfort. One day I'd like to shove a cricket bat up his arse and see how he feels about it! Anyway, I could have told him my temperature was way high as this whole experience was making my blood boil.

To be continued…

FEBRUARY 27

Dear diary,

The trip to the torture chamber, part five. After the torturer removed his thermometer from my intimate area, he decided to weigh me. So, reluctantly, I allowed myself to be put on the scales. I really wish I hadn't. His tut was loud enough to break the ice and he proceeded to tell my humans that I'd put on weight. How dare you, I thought. Okay, maybe I've filled out a little since the last time but I'm big-boned and it's mainly muscle. Next, he's telling them to cut back on the food and limit the treats!

Oh, God, can this day get any worse?

Of course, the answer is yes and before I know what's coming, he's got hold of a bunch of skin at the back of my neck and has stabbed me. "I thought you were supposed to only do good." The final element of the torture soon followed as he prized my jaw open and inserted this foul-tasting tablet. Well, diary, I nearly gagged. Please let that be the end of it, I thought.

To be continued…

FEBRUARY 28

Dear diary,

This is the final entry about the trip to the torture chamber,
I promise, probably. Well, after so much physical and emotional
abuse, boy was I glad to get back into the relative safety of the
lunar module. We were soon back in the waiting room while he
paid, and then, I might add, grumbled about the size of the bill all
the way home. So why do it to me, if you are only going to bitch
about how much it cost? Trust me, I'm not getting anything from
it. When we got home, I was expecting to be spoilt to make up
for the pain and suffering I had endured, but it seems they only
remembered the incident on the scales and there were slim pickings
for supper and no treats.

I will have to go out later and
get a takeaway.

It's so unfair.

MARCH 1

Dear diary,

My recent trip to the torture chamber has given me further insight into the working of the minds of dogs and, diary, it's not a terribly pretty picture. I know that any trip to the vets is going to be a ghastly experience and no good is going to come from it. The humans arrange it and take me there, so I am in no doubt about who is ultimately to blame for my mental and physical suffering. But what I don't get is why dogs don't understand the process. I've watched them as they come out of the torture chamber to be reunited with their humans and they're all wagging their tails and jumping up with excitement.

Wake up and smell the coffee, dogs! Your humans brought you here so you could suffer. Instead of trying to lick their faces, I'd at least take a piss up their legs to show my true feelings.

Have some self-respect, please.

MARCH 6

Dear diary,

I feel like I need to get something down on paper. It is one of the most distressing incidents of my life and happened when I was a kitten, but I still bear the emotional scars. She decided that a cat flap operated by a magnet would be the best way for me to get in and out of the house. Okay by me, I thought at the time. What I didn't realise was that I would be required to wear a collar with a small magnet attached in order to operate the flap while keeping other cats locked out. Well, cats are not like dogs and we do not like wearing collars. I protested loudly but was rather brusquely over-ruled. The collar stayed. To be continued…

MARCH 7

Dear diary,

The collar, part two. Well, I felt a right jessie wearing this collar and tried my hardest to wriggle out of it, but to no avail. The only flipside was that I was free to come and go as I liked. However, on the second day I had a truly terrifying experience that still leaves me shaking when I think about it. I was pottering around the kitchen when I must have got closer to the fridge door than previously. Without warning, I was dragged sideways at an alarming speed until the magnet locked onto the fridge door. I was trapped and did not have the strength to pull away. I called for help, but the house was empty. I don't know how long I was trapped, but I think I was drifting in and out of consciousness at one point. Finally, after what seemed hours, she came home and upon realising my predicament, promptly burst out laughing. That was not the reaction I expected. Once set free, I didn't know whether to have a drink or a wee first. Frankly, I was very disappointed at her reaction. The only good thing to come out of the ordeal was that the magnet and collar idea was dropped forthwith.

MARCH 14

Dear diary,

The lane past our house is a remarkably
busy thoroughfare at times as the great
and the good of the village take the air.
This can be in the form of walking with
loved ones, walking with someone else's
loved ones, walking the dog or dogs, jogging,
cycling or sometimes, it seems, simply standing in
the middle of the road flapping gums with neighbours. I see it all,
when I'm awake in daylight hours, from several different vantage
points and I have awarded nicknames to some of the regulars. In
no particular order, we have characters like Nervous Nellie, Lardy
Dog, the Shuffling Jogger and Scary Woman. I have to admit
that Nervous Nellie is my favourite as she can be made to jump
at the sight of her own shadow and I've perfected a little stunt I
pull on her from time to time. When I see her coming, I take up
a position just behind the wall and then at the last moment leap
out sideways, hissing and all fluffed up to make me look as big and
scary as possible. It never fails! While I leg it to safety, she heads
home for another dose of valium and gin.

MARCH 18

Dear diary,

Sometimes I can even get into trouble just by taking a nap. I came back in the other morning after a night patrol and, okay I admit, I was a bit grubby. I'd picked up some mud on my paws and some bits and pieces of undergrowth were caught up in my fur. But unlike a dog, I was perfectly happy to sort it out myself and didn't expect the humans to get me cleaned up. I thought they would have been pleased with my self-cleaning abilities but I was wrong. I found a comfy spot in the utility room on top of the laundry basket and set about a vigorous cleaning session. Once complete, I settled down for a very pleasant sleep. Well, you should have heard the fuss when she came in and found me. Apparently, she'd just washed and ironed the contents of the basket and a little bit of mud and a twig or two had ruined it. Honestly, I think she over-reacted rather badly. Maybe it's that time of the month…

MARCH 23

Dear diary,

It's so unfair. They eat chips, Sunday roasts, takeaways, chocolate and ice cream on a pretty regular basis. I get the same boring tinned cat food, a few dry biscuits and water. If I'm lucky, every couple of weeks I might get a few cat treats. I am becoming increasingly concerned about the lack of variety in my diet — particularly the lack of cat treats and tuna. But how do I get them to understand what I am trying to tell them?

What would Lassie do in a situation like this?

(best angelic face)

Please feed me...

MARCH 26

Dear diary,

War has broken out! This house is no longer a safe place for an emotionally fragile cat. The man of the house went out with some mates last night and came back in a rather intoxicated state. I watched the whole sorry pantomime from a hiding place in the front garden. After a lot of staggering about, he managed to find his door key but couldn't get it into the key hole. Instead, and this was dreadfully ill-advised, he rang the doorbell. Now, she'd been in bed for about an hour at this point and was clearly not amused at being disturbed. But he had his beer goggles on and made a lunge for her as he tripped over the milk bottles and stumbled into the hallway. From what I can piece together, his amorous advances continued up the stairs but she was having none of it and he was promptly banished to the spare room. The atmosphere this morning can best be described as frosty. He's trying to make amends and is only succeeding in making it worse.

I am thinking about having an anxiety attack.

MARCH 27

Dear diary,

Following last night's dramas when he came home drunk,
I have revisited my panic room as I thought I was going to need
it. My panic room is, in fact, a dark back corner of the airing
cupboard that I found a while ago. With a little squeeze and
wriggle I can get into a corner that no one but me knows about.
My only slight concern is that the access seems to have become a
little tighter since I last visited and I'm a bit worried that I'll get
in there and not be able to get back out again. No one would ever
know I was there and would they hear my calls for help?

APRIL 2

Dear diary,

There is a chap down the road called Trevor, who keeps chickens in his back garden. Sometimes he has so many eggs that he puts a little table on the side of the road and sells the surplus stock. It's straight out of "The Good Life" and he seems harmless and happy enough. However, what has come to rather trouble me is that he talks to the chickens. He's given them names and regularly proclaims his love for them. Maybe he wasn't breastfed as a child or perhaps Mrs Trevor isn't quite the bedroom performer that she was 40 years ago. Given that she has a five o-clock shadow first thing in the morning and is seldom seen without an apron and curlers, that's not so hard to imagine. My view is that Trevor has transferred the focus of his love to his chickens. From now on, I shall call him the chicken whisperer.

APRIL 4

Dear diary,

Next door to us lives a dog.

Small.

Yappy.

Annoying!

Okay, I admit that I really don't get dogs. They seem to have the memory of a forgetful goldfish and spend way too much time trying to please their humans. Why? All that excitement when the humans come home really sends out all the wrong signals. I really can't fathom why any animal is so keen to have a lead put around its neck and be taken outside for a walk twice a day, even on the coldest and wettest days. If I want to go outside, I hop through the flap and have a mooch around. Why isn't it the same for dogs? Letting yourself out and taking a walk seems the sensible thing to do. Even when they get taken for a walk, it always seems like a battle of wills. Either the dog is straining against the lead to go further or faster or being pulled along when it clearly can't be arsed to go for a walk. The whole thing makes no sense.

APRIL 5

Dear diary,

So help me, if I can get hold of a gun, that yappy dog next door is going to be rubbed out. I like to catch up on my sleep during the day and it is becoming increasingly difficult due to Fido's constant racket. It barks when they are in, it barks when they are out, it barks when they leave and it barks when they get back. What are you trying to tell us, dog? You really need to up your game on non-verbal communication because at the moment you are sending out terribly mixed messages.

Trust me, if I can get hold of a gun, you're going to be a hot-water bottle cover in pretty short order.

APRIL 8

Dear diary,

We have some very strange neighbours. Very strange, indeed.

In one of the bigger houses lives Roger and his wife. I can't even remember her name as she keeps such a low profile, but I have discovered that neither of them like cats. I've had abuse, and items of gardening equipment, thrown at me whenever I've been spotted in their manicured grounds.

Of course, knowing that my presence winds them up makes it all so much more worthwhile. There's nothing quite as satisfying as taking a healthy dump in neatly prepared flower beds and hoping they'll find my calling card the next day.

APRIL 10

Dear diary,

Becalmed.

That's how I feel today. The weather is still, the house is still.
Even the neighbours, and that annoying little dog, seem to
have gone quiet for once.

I feel like I am floating on a sea of tranquillity and my chakras
are aligned. Peace and love, man, peace and love.

APRIL 13

Dear diary,

I'm going to share one of my innermost secrets today. I know I go on about the humans and I can tend to moan a bit, but as in the words of the song "Just let me say for the record", I really am terribly fond of them. One of my favourite places is curled up on his lap while he snoozes in front of the tellybox. He seems to generate such a lot of warmth, not all of it through farting, that it is one of my happy places. The same goes for her; if I can sneak onto the bed and curl up beside her early in the morning, it is a special moment. Of course, I can't afford to let this go on for too long as it is breakfast time!

There, I said it. Please don't see me as weak.

APRIL 17

Dear diary,

Back to the topic of Roger next door. It is, dear diary, a cruel irony that his parents had to christen Roger long before he was able to speak, for he is stricken with a most pronounced speech impediment. He can't say his Rs, which is such a blow when you are called Roger. If they'd called him Tom or Dave or something like that, his life would have been so much easier. However, this is manna for a cat who has been on the receiving end of a good deal of unpleasantness from him and his wife, so in my head they will forever be Wodga and Mrs Wodga!

APRIL 19

Dear diary,

Modern life is alarming and confusing. I try not to watch the news as it is generally bleak and disturbing.

I think the BBC has a master plan to keep us all running scared most of the time. However, there are also things that confuse me and, in no particular order, I simply do not understand Ikea adverts, most of the presenters on Radio 2 and The Kardashians. None of them seem to bear any resemblance to reality and are simply superfluous. A bit like tits on fish, I reckon.

APRIL 23

We've had a security breach. I wandered into the kitchen earlier on for a light snack and that fat ginger tom from down the road was helping himself to MY food. I was incensed! Somehow, he'd squeezed his portly frame through my door and there he was, bold as brass, stealing the food from my tray. I was so taken aback that I was rendered largely speechless, but I did give him a hard stare. He sort of took the hint and waddled back to the door and, after a lot of huffing, puffing and wriggling, managed to get back out. My last sight of him was of his huge arse escaping through my door. I was appalled and need to carefully consider my next move. In fact, I think I'll sleep on it. But be warned, 'Ginge', this is war.

APRIL 26

Dear diary,

I'm still stinging from the comments made by the vet about my weight. However, I'm rather distressed to have to admit that he might have a point. I caught sight of my reflection in the glass kitchen door this morning and, while there is no denying my fine feline physique, it is possible that I've added a little timber here and there. Now, humans and dogs do exercise, which is such a waste of energy and simply not for us cats. But maybe I'm going to have to put the brakes on calorie intake a little and I'll have to start with takeaways. You know what they say about a mouse: a moment on the lips and a lifetime on the hips.

Oh dear, there are dark days ahead.

APRIL 30

Dear diary,

Well, I decided on a strategy to deal with raids from Ginge and I have to say it all worked beautifully. I do like it when a plan comes together! I decided I had to hit hard and hit fast in order to stop him coming in and cleaning up my food. Judging by the size of him, he's not exactly being underfed at home. So, I took up position in the kitchen, hidden from his view, and it wasn't long before I heard him outside, starting to haul his bulk up to push through the flap. I waited just long enough for his nose to fully appear before launching my attack. With claws on maximum extension I leapt across the kitchen and delivered a mighty swipe to his nose. I was like a ninja! He let out a mighty yelp and rapidly engaged reverse. He just didn't know what had hit him. I know I drew blood as, on later examination, there were traces of blood around the flap. I last saw him wobbling away as fast as his legs could carry him. Result!

MAY 3

Dear diary,

He's just got home from the supermarket. It is his weekly
contribution to domestic chores and he's always terribly proud
of himself. I think it might be some throwback to primeval
times when the hunter gatherer would bring home a woolly
mammoth for the family to feast upon. But I don't imagine his
life was much in peril as he pushed his trolley along the frozen
food aisle. The frozen turkeys were not likely to launch a vicious
counter-attack as he stalked some chips. However, he seems
proud of himself.

I just hope he remembered the cat treats and tuna.

MAY 4

Dear diary,

I have found the perfect place to rest a while on a cold night in early spring — the roof of next door's garden shed! I know, it seems highly implausible that the roof of a garden shed on a cold night could nearly be too warm, but that's what I found when I hopped up there last night. The heat coming from inside the shed was wonderful and I took advantage by having a little catnap. But while lying there enjoying the warmth, it got me wondering. Why does Wodga keep his shed so warm and why has he got three padlocks on the door?

Then, with a flash of understanding, the answer hit me. He's growing tomatoes for the village summer fair and he wants to get a head start on the opposition. Judging by the heat escaping from that shed, he's going to have tomatoes the size of footballs by July!

MAY 6

Dear diary,

The Lord giveth and the Lord taketh away. That's just how it is. Early this morning, the Lord took from Trevor the chicken whisperer and gave to me. Never look a gift horse in the mouth (whatever that means). I was heading home a little later than usual and was skirting Trevor's back garden when I saw him out there, proclaiming undying love to his coop. They obviously enjoy the love and had been busy, so he had a nice basket of eggs gathered up ready to take back into the house. Unfortunately, there was a rather late frost and he took a spectacular fall as he tottered back inside in his slippers. The eggs went everywhere and most smashed on the ground.

So, while poor Trevor hobbled into the house clutching his back, I took full advantage as a raw egg or three is a real treat. He was gone for some time, doubtless hoping that Mrs Trevor would rub it better. But looking at her from a safe distance, it's probably a very long time since she rubbed any part of his anatomy.

MAY 9

Dear diary,

I'm in big trouble. I'll call it 'Pigeon-gate'. I went outside this afternoon for a mooch around and spied a pigeon on the lawn. Now I don't rate pigeons as being the smartest of birds and so I slowly crept up behind 'Walter' without him even realising I was there. So, I jumped him and quickly took control as he squawked a bit. Now what to do? Well, maybe on reflection this wasn't my smartest idea, but I decided to take him inside as a present for the humans to show them how clever I was. It was a bit of an effort getting this bird through the cat flap, but I managed it. But then, to be honest, I got a bit bored with the whole idea and let go of it while I thought about where to go for a nap.

How could I have known that Walter would now go completely mental and start flying around the kitchen, squawking, leaving feathers all over the place and pooing at an alarming rate on all the work tops? I legged it but the humans were very cross when they got home and they have clearly decided it was all my fault.

Walter, looking a little dishevelled, was eventually released back to the garden.

MAY 11

Dear diary,

The turf war with Ginge has taken an unpleasant turn. His retaliation to my ninja attack on his nose was to leave a turd right outside my cat flap. It was mahoosive! I'd never have believed that any cat could deliver such a turd. He must be feeding in every house on the street to build up a 'Richard the third' of such a scale. It fair took my breath away when I saw it. I just hope I don't get the blame when the humans come home.

I hope they remember the old saying about not pooing on your own doorstep. I'd also hate to think they'd consider me capable of producing such a vast jobby.

MAY 14

Dear diary,

Just down the road is a very odd man. He wears a lot of beige and drives a Honda Jazz. I can only assume that he is a geography teacher and I suspect he lives on his own. However, despite his unrelenting dullness, I've discovered that he can be a first class source of entertainment. Every Sunday morning he parks the Jazz on the drive and washes it with all the care and attention he can muster. He then polishes it to within an inch of its life, before standing back to admire his efforts. When he heads inside for what I presume will be a cup of tea and a celebratory digestive as a special treat, it is time to pounce. I find a muddy puddle, which is not difficult given the amount of water he has sprayed over his beloved Honda. I get all four paws as muddy as I can and then do a slow walk up over the bonnet, front windscreen, roof, rear window and tailgate. It is a work of art, and he shows his appreciation by leaping up and down, throwing his chamois on the ground and kicking his bucket of water all over the drive. Of course, I watch this little pantomime from a safe location. It really does make a quiet Sunday morning most enjoyable.

MAY 17

Dear diary,

To quote a famous
Billy Connolly line:
"My arse is in tatters."

Let me explain. The family had a
takeaway curry last night. When they'd
finished, as usual, they stacked the plates in the
kitchen and settled down for a snooze and a fart on the sofa.
When they cleared off to bed, I went for a poke around the
leftovers as I'm quite partial to a bit of chicken korma. I spied
what I thought was korma and tucked in enthusiastically and I'd
swallowed a couple of mouthfuls before it hit me. This was not a
korma. This was something up there in vindaloo territory! I dived
for the water bowl but it was too late. My mouth was on fire and,
in pretty short order, so was my arse! It burned going in and it
burned coming out. No wonder they didn't eat it all…

Lesson learned.

MAY 21

Dear diary,

I think I've become an ornithologist. The other weekend, the humans put up a bird feeder in the garden full of the little treats and snacks that birds like. I do question why no one has come up with the idea of cat feeders. Anyway, I digress. From a comfortable position on the back of the sofa, I can watch my little feathered friends coming and going and being terribly busy. In fact, it makes me feel tired just watching them, so the thought of going out and trying to catch one leaves me quite exhausted.

I think I'll just watch from a distance and then have a little snooze when they tire me out.

MAY 23

Dear diary,

I've not mentioned Old Bert before, so perhaps I should now as he's a grumpy old bastard who clearly does not like cats. He's got a row of teeth like a burnt fence, speaks in some weird long-forgotten local dialect and must be 100 years old. He also seems to be made of kryptonite as he just goes on and on.

The neighbours try to talk to him, but I'm convinced they never understand a word he says. My female human said hello to him the other evening and I swear his reply was: "Yer, mangle wurzel be bust so happen Fat Larry's Band and they turnips be gurning." She clearly didn't have a clue what he said but nodded enthusiastically and said she had something in the oven and had better be going, which was a complete tissue of lies.

MAY 29

Dear diary

I am bored.

I am soooooooo bored.

The humans have all gone out for the day. I've had a snooze and I've had a dump and now I'm bored.

I wish something exciting would happen.

I may have a potter round next door and see if Wodga is up to some mischief.

JUNE 1

Dear diary,

I'm on the lookout for a hired assassin. I've decided that the time has come to put a contract on the head of Ginge. Ever since he left the massive turd on our doormat, he's been taunting me and I'm getting tired of it. If I ever encounter him on my travels, he's developed a most unpleasant habit of turning around, lifting his tail and showing me his bottom. Yes, thank you, I know where the offending item was produced. I am now worried that this turf war is going to escalate further and if it turns nasty, I don't think he will fight fair. So, the time has come for him to be terminated. But I need to find a hired gun to do the deed. I wonder if there are any advertising in the village magazine amongst the plumbers and general handymen? A man who is handy with a .22 rifle would do perfectly.

JUNE 2

Dear diary,

Let's return to a favourite topic — Wodga next door.

I think I've discovered that he's a wrong 'un and the evidence is pretty compelling. Recently, the humans were gossiping about him fiddling the village Christmas Club accounts, as he'd apparently trousered some of the cash that people were saving up to spend on Christmas. Then, the lead on the church roof went missing and I reckon he was involved. I see a lot of stuff going on outside the hours of daylight and he keeps having late night visits from some dodgy looking characters. I think he sees himself as the Don Corleone of the village, controlling organised crime, dealing drugs and nicking Christmas cash off the pensioners. From now on, I shall call him Wodga the Wobba. Maybe he's stealing to fund the drink- and drugs-fuelled lifestyle of Mrs Wodga.

It's becoming a fascinating insight into what lurks behind the net curtains of rural life — outwardly caring members of the community, but inwardly as morally corrupt as a politician in the build-up to an election.

JUNE 5

Dear diary,

I have a most interesting development to report.

Well, it's more of a puzzle really. Last night, when the humans stopped snoring on the sofa, turned the tellybox off and went to bed, I ventured outside for a patrol of the neighbourhood. It was a pleasantly warm evening with a full moon.

Anyway, I heard laughter coming from a few doors down and went for a look. It was the house of a youngish couple who seem very popular and have quite a few friends in the village. There is a fence around the garden which offers the perfect place to see into the dining room but without being seen.

So, I hopped up to see what all the fun was about. Inside were four couples having what seemed to be a very jolly dinner party. Judging by the number of empty wine bottles being dumped outside the kitchen door, it was all going swimmingly.

To be continued…

JUNE 6

Dear diary,

On closer inspection of the
dinner party, I recognised
four couples from the village.
I'll call them couple A, couple B, couple C and couple D, although
their real names are Barrington, Harvey, Grimble and Duckett so
they sound like a firm of lawyers. Anyway, they were clearly getting
through the supermarket Merlot at a fair old rate. But, I reasoned,
no harm would be done as they could all walk home with no
need to drive. I was about to continue my patrol, when it became
apparent that the dinner party was breaking up, so I decided to
stay put until they'd cleared off home.

And that's when it all got rather puzzling.

JUNE 7

Dear diary,

Imagine my surprise when the first pair to emerge from the front door were Mr A and Mrs C. That's odd, I thought. Perhaps he's going to be a gentleman and walk her home as she's had one too many glasses of red. But if he was helping her in a slightly intoxicated state, surely it would have been safer to put his hand on her arm rather than firmly on her bottom. But she didn't seem to mind in the least and was whispering to him as they headed up the road.

Probably telling him the latest gossip about Wodga, I surmised.

JUNE 8

Dear diary,

Well, curiouser and curiouser. Next to leave the dinner party were Mr D and Mrs B and she must have been feeling chilly as she'd got his jacket wrapped around her as they headed the other way towards her house. Finally, Mr C and Mrs D came out arm in arm, which left Mrs A and Mr B in her house and they didn't seem to be leaving. In fact, almost straightaway the upstairs lights went on and I could hear giggling from the stairs. I guess he'd had a bit too much to drink and was going to sleep it off. But the whole situation left many unanswered questions.

Several hours later, the plot thickened further when Mr B left quietly by the back door and a few minutes later Mr A came back down the road and let himself in his own front door.

It's all very strange and if it is some new form of party game, I really don't get it.

JUNE 10

Dear diary,

I'm sorry but I just can't be bothered to write anything. If I'm honest, I've been feeling a bit down lately and so I'm just going to spend the day restoring my emotional balance.

Food and sleep should help to restore my karma.

I may even light some joss sticks. I need some me time.

JUNE 11

Dear diary,

I almost felt sorry for Trevor the chicken whisperer today. I was having a lunchtime perambulate when I heard shouting and screaming from his kitchen. This was all rather interesting I thought and inched a little closer. Well, it seems that Mrs Trevor was a tiny bit cross and was giving him the benefit of her opinion. It appears that his heinous crime was to walk across her freshly mopped kitchen floor in his gardening shoes. He was getting both barrels and Mrs Trevor, with mad starey eyes and bits of phlegm bursting from her mouth, was a truly scary proposition. Let's just say that she had her loving, gentle, feminine side completely under control.

Now I understand why he showers so much love on his chickens.

JUNE 12

Dear diary,

I shall continue the story of Trevor and Mrs Trevor. Once she'd finished lambasting him for daring to get mud on her kitchen floor, she clearly needed a moment or two of mindfulness and relaxation to restore her inner calm.

Now, in our house that would involve, in varying degrees, a candle-lit bath, red wine and chocolate followed by a rom-com on the tellybox. But Mrs Trevor is clearly a different type of woman. Very shortly she appeared from the kitchen and headed to the shed where she fired up the diesel generator, put on her welding mask and goggles and started doing some therapeutic metalwork. Formidable is the word that springs to mind. I think Trevor has gone to hide with his chickens for a few days.

JUNE 13

Dear diary,

I shall return to the subject of Old Bert after a rather ugly incident first thing this morning. I was on my way home across his front garden when I received a very urgent call of nature. I just had time to find a corner of freshly dug earth in his vegetable garden before nature arrived and it was with some relief that I avoided an embarrassing indiscretion.

However, I'd barely had time to cover up the offending item when I heard Old Bert approaching. At least I assumed, correctly as it turned out, that it was Old Bert. "Yer cooking fat, thees dursn't doberrry on me marrows, thee turnip bashing carburettor." Well, that's what it sounded like.

Far more worrying was a surprisingly well-aimed pitchfork that whistled past my ear as I made my escape. Crazy old gimmer!

JUNE 17

Dear diary,

I had a most interesting foray into next door's garden last night and what a spectacle I was lucky enough to behold! I was pottering quietly about in the flower beds when I spied an odd shape on the lawn. Upon closer inspection, I discovered it was Mrs Wodga in what can best be described as a state of considerable intoxication. Okay, she was completely plastered and lying face down on the grass, dribbling and mumbling incoherently. The empty gin bottle in her right hand told its own tragic story.

Well, this was truly bounty from on high and I found a nice, secluded spot in the begonias and settled down to see what developed. I didn't have to wait long! A few minutes later, Wodga emerged from the front door, calling for his beloved and shining a torch around. From the tone of his voice, I detected that he was perhaps a little cross.

My powers of observation were soon to be proved correct. When he spotted the miscreant on the lawn, he rushed off and came back with the garden hose and promptly gave her a good soaking, presumably to go with the one she'd already had! I honestly didn't

think there was any risk of her catching fire but the hosing down was most thorough. Once she had emerged from her tired and emotional state and realised what was happening, she made it abundantly clear that she was not happy with the outcome. The shouting, bad language and banging of doors went on for quite some time.

Oh, diary, this pair is the gift that keeps on giving; this was a most enjoyable night!

JUNE 19

Dear diary,

I want to write about ADHD. I was curled up with the humans the other night and was only paying limited notice of the tellybox when something caught my interest. The presenters were talking about Attention Deficit Hyperactivity Disorder in kids. Now, the hyperactive bit was of no interest to me, but the attention deficit bit really grabbed my notice.

Suddenly it all became clear and it was like a spotlight being turned on. All these years, I've suffered in silence, but now there is a proper name for what I suffer with each and every day. I have attention deficit disorder.

I just hope the humans were paying attention and will now commence a rigorous course of therapy to give me the attention I have clearly needed for some time.

JUNE 21

Dear diary,

I am at a low ebb.

I feel fat and unloved.

I'm going to sleep, eat and repeat.

I'm not available for anyone or anything today.

JUNE 22

Dear diary,

I feel very peculiar indeed and it's taken me a little while to figure
it out. I was patrolling next door's garden last night when I heard
some giggling coming from the shed. I crept a little nearer to
see what was going on and I could hear Wodga and Mrs Wodga
talking in hushed voices between bouts of giggling. But what really
got my attention was the strange smelling smoke coming out of
the shed windows. At first I thought the silly fools were having an
in-door barbecue, perhaps involving potentially award-winning
tomatoes, so I quietly hopped up onto the roof to take a sniff.
But this wasn't the smell of sausages and burgers, and once I'd
taken a couple of lung fulls, I identified a musky smell with a hint
of skunk.

I very soon felt rather light-headed. Somehow, I got off the shed
roof and back home in relative safety, but on the way I encountered
two large elephants, a juggler on a unicycle and a fire-breathing
dragon. I now know the smell was marijuana and I'd been on a
different sort of trip. A most odd sensation.

Naughty Wodga!

JUNE 24

Dear diary,

I've just reread a few of my recent diary entries and I'm a little concerned that I might be coming over as rather short-tempered and intolerant. Of course, nothing could be further from the truth. I'm a placid, easy-going cat who just wants to live a peaceful life and sleep most of the day. But if anyone disturbs me, they'll get it! I have many tools at my disposal for showing my displeasure when I'm driven to the end of my tether by noise and disturbance. I can choose from an arsenal that includes sicking up a fur ball, taking a dump in a favourite pair of slippers or simply clawing my way up the side of the sofa. So just beware a sleep-deprived cat.

JUNE 27

Dear diary,

The turf war has reared its ugly head again.

Ginge, the huge tom from down the road, has decided to renew his efforts to unsettle me and has taken to creeping up on me when I least expect it. I can be catching some rays under a bush in someone's garden and he'll suddenly be behind me doing an impression of Hannibal Lecter and it completely freaks me out. I'm pretty sure he's not into feline cannibalism, but he's definitely got me rattled. I have no wish to reprise the role of Clarice.

JUNE 30

Dear diary,

Well diary, I've finally discovered something interesting about
Mr Beige Honda Jazz man. It seems he likes to keep fish and has a
substantial fish pool set up in his back garden. I know this because
I was having a nose around the other night and nearly jumped
out of my skin when one of the blighters did a massive jump and
landed on the ground beside the pool. I don't think he meant to
do that! Well, never one to miss an opportunity, I saw a chance to
demonstrably show my love for my humans. After all, she is always
wittering on about having more fish in their diet.

To be continued…

JULY 1

Dear diary,

So, here I was presented with a flapping fish and a golden opportunity. It was a case of seize the day — carpe diem — or perhaps that should be carp diem.

So I seized both the day and the carp and jumped the fish. It was a bit big to carry, but I managed to get a grip on it and set off home, imagining how pleased the humans would be with my catch.

I could almost taste the cat treats over the general fishiness. Getting the slippery bugger through the cat flap was a challenge but I managed with a bit of a wrestle and took it upstairs to show them!

To be continued…

JULY 2

Dear diary,

Carpgate part three. I hopped up onto the bed to show them my prize but just as I did, the damn thing got away from me and landed back on the floor before jumping under the bed. That was not how I'd planned it. I dived under the bed to try and regain control of Colin the carp just as she woke up, turned the light on and looked under the bed to see what all the commotion was about.

She seemed quite surprised by what she saw and shouted: "There's a live fish under the bed!" This woke him up, as he rolled half over and said: "You're having a bad dream — throw it out of the window." He then rolled back over and went back to sleep.

See part four…

JULY 3

Dear diary,

Part four: so, there we were — her, Colin and me in a bit of a Mexican stand-off. I decided my work was done. I'd delivered fresh fish and it was up to her to deal with it now, so I legged it. I'm not sure what she did with Colin but I certainly got the cold shoulder in the morning and I don't think the man of the house was much in favour either. There really is no pleasing some people.

I never did get a nice bit of cooked fish as a reward for my sterling effort and I don't think they had filet of fish for supper either.

I don't think I'll try it again. Next time, if she wants fresh fish, she'll have to go to Sainsbury's.

JULY 5

Dear diary,

I am utterly soaked. I've even got water inside my ears and it has probably gone up my bum as well. How did this happen? That miserable, cat-hating, scrote, Old Bert, that's how. I knew he was out and about fussing over his vegetables but I thought I was out of reach. Sadly, I had badly miscalculated and was still within range of his garden hose. For a fossil, he is surprisingly nimble on his feet and before I had time to dive for cover I took a direct hit from a ferocious jet of water. It was a deeply unpleasant experience and a combination of the shock and the cold water rather took my breath away.

As I recovered some composure and legged it, I could hear him taunting me and shouting what sounded like: "Ha, ha, lardy cat. You'm copped it up the back passage! Ha, ha, I'll 'ave 'ee Mungo Jerry puss, puss."

JULY 9

Dear diary,

This summer weather
really is taking the piss.
It is 30 degrees outside and
simply too hot. I just cannot
be arsed to write anything.

I've even got sweaty paws.

Later…

JULY 11

Dear diary,

I had a dream. Not in the style of Martin Luther King, of course, but it was definitely a dream and I was most disappointed to wake up from it.

I actually think it was more of a premonition. It involved Wodga the Wobba being busted by a heavily armed SWAT team and it was epic. I saw it all! A helicopter suddenly appeared overhead with a massive search light and several big 4x4s skidded to a halt on the drive, scattering gravel all over the freshly mown lawn and full of men in combat kit carrying automatic guns. Then this big booming voice through a loud hailer came down from the helicopter saying: "Come out with your hands up Wodga, we've got you suwwounded! Put down your garden fawk and lie down on the gwass. Wesistance is futile."

I was loving it when I did a little fart and woke myself up and I was gutted when I realised it was all a dream. But your time will come, Wodga, your time will come!

JULY 14

Dear diary,

I've scored a victory over Big Ginge.
I do like it when a plan comes together!

From recent bitter experience, I've got a good handle on the range
of Old Bert's garden hose. So I positioned myself carefully and
waited for Ginge to creep up behind me on one of his Hannibal
missions. He was blissfully unaware of what he was
about to get. I let him get into the ideal spot and then
leapt into the air, making myself as large and noisy as
possible before diving off the wall into a safe zone.
Old Bert was just watering his string beans when
he heard me but spotted Ginge and duly delivered
a direct hit. Ginge didn't even see it coming
but the forceful jet of water knocked
him off the wall in a bedraggled heap.
He never knew what hit him!

Oh, how I laughed. There is a god,
after all. Just for this once, well done
Old Bert.

JULY 16

Dear diary,

Well, that didn't pan out the
way I hoped it would. I was
having an early evening mooch around the garden and spotted
a frog hopping about. In what seemed like a brilliant idea at the
time, I thought I'd catch it and take it home for everyone to see.

On considered reflection, I can now see that perhaps it wasn't
such a smart move. However, I jumped the jumper and took him
through the cat flap. I have to say that frogs don't taste very nice
but I thought my reward would come once the humans saw how
clever I'd been.

What I didn't anticipate was that Freddie Frog would start
squealing like a stuck pig as soon as I deposited him on the kitchen
floor. His racket was soon rivalled by her squawking as it all
suddenly got out of hand.

While the humans chased Freddie around the kitchen, I made
a quick exit to reflect on what I'd done. A sort of self-imposed
naughty step.

JULY 17

Dear diary,

The story of Wodga's shed continues!

Now that I've realised it is in fact a marijuana factory, I'm keeping a particular eye on it. On a chilly night it is the perfect place to rest a while and warm up, as the roof is always very warm — sometimes too warm! Of course, I've also realised why Wodga flatly refuses to take part in the annual village 'open garden' weekend. While the other villagers are welcoming perfect strangers into their gardens and feeding them cream teas, Wodga glares at everyone over his gate and makes it abundantly clear that his garden is not open!

He clearly doesn't want the terminally nosy inspecting his more exotic plants.

JULY 20

Dear diary,

Don't get me started on courier drivers.

We live in a pretty quiet lane, but it's sometimes like Silverstone when the courier drivers are on the job. I blame my humans for some of the problem as she orders a lot of stuff on a well-known internet site. Each one of those orders results in a loud bang on the door, usually when I've just settled down for a well-earned daytime sleep. The courier drivers just don't seem to be able to do anything quietly. From screeching to a halt, banging on the door, shouting about the parcel and then departing by revving the good old diesel Transit to 4000rpm in every gear, the whole experience is aural torture for a sleepy cat.

To make it worse, very seldom has she bought anything for me.

JULY 21

Dear diary,

On the topic of Wodga and the open garden weekend, I've had
a great idea. Instead of offering cream teas or glasses of hideous
homemade wine, Wodga could join in and offer day visits
to the hordes of nosy gits who turn out for the annual open
garden weekend.

He could show them around his garden, then invite them into
his shed and give them a sample spliff to try. I'm sure they'd
all enjoy themselves and queue up to place orders for further
supplies. It's a brilliant marketing idea for his exotic plants.

Then, the sight of all the visitors roaming the village completely
off their faces would really make it a weekend to remember!

JULY 23

Dear diary,

I have discovered a great new game. Normally, if I bring a mouse into the house for a play date they have a habit of diving under the sofa where I can't get at them. That's no fun at all. But by chance the other night I found a way of preventing that.

Let them go in the bath! You've now got a captive audience and you can chase them around until you lose interest. It's brilliant!

Sadly, the humans don't seem to share my enthusiasm for this new night-time game and last night I took a direct hit on the back of the head from a well-aimed slipper. I consider that to have been a bit of an over-reaction but it's not going to stop me playing my new favourite game again.

JULY 27

Dear diary,

I'm having a bad fur day.

On my way home this morning, I managed to brush past a dreaded burr plant without realising and now I have several of the little blighters firmly embedded in my fur.

It's vital that I ferret them out before she gets home otherwise I know what will happen. She'll get the scissors out and hack off great lumps of fur, leaving me looking like an old teddy bear who has seen better days.

Lord, this would all be a lot easier if only I had opposing thumbs.

JULY 29

Dear diary,

Today I'd like to write about tuna. It is a favourite subject of mine, yet there seems to be a distinct lack of it in this house. It is a source of quality protein and is just about fat-free. It contains essential amino acids and tinned tuna is a good source of omega 3 fatty acids, which are good for your heart.

And I like it, a lot.

So why do the humans not recognise this and serve it up to me more often instead of the same old, same old cat food. God only knows what is in some of those tins.

Is anyone listening to me? Tuna is available in all leading supermarkets.

AUGUST 1

Dear diary,

I am a bit worried. I believe there is an axis of evil forming in our road and it seems to be aimed squarely at me. From what little intelligence I can gather, it seems that Old Bert and Trevor the chicken whisperer have formed an unholy alliance to gang up on me. Clearly Trevor does not like me upsetting his chickens and I'm certainly not welcome in Bert's vegetable garden. Stronger together seems to be their motto and I've recently seen them trading eggs for marrows. When they spotted me, there was a lot of pointing and gesticulating in my direction along with some rather choice words although, as usual, Bert made little sense. They seemed to be rather enjoying themselves until Mrs Trevor opened her front door and ordered Trevor inside.

I need to be vigilant.

AUGUST 7

Dear diary,

The family has gone on holiday, again… I know this because they made a big fuss of me one day and then the suitcases were by the front door and then it all went quiet. Then, each day for a week, some random Herbert has appeared to open a tin, throw some biscuits in the bowl and splash some milk around.

It really is not good enough and if I were a human child, I'd have good reason to call social services. Instead, I am left to roam the house, bereft and alone, trying to cope with major separation issues.

Actually, that last bit isn't entirely true. I rather like the peace and quiet and being able to sleep wherever I want, whenever I want, even if food availability is somewhat below my usual expectations.

I expect they'll be back soon enough, tired, sun burnt and arguing, ready to bring their own special brand of chaos back to the house.

AUGUST 15

Dear diary,

As I predicted they have returned. They've clearly been somewhere hot and sunny as he looks like a beetroot and she's dancing around the kitchen singing "Agadoo". My peace and tranquillity have been well and truly shattered. As usual, in these situations, I was faced with a difficult choice. Should I hide out for 24 hours to get them worried and feeling guilty, should I show utter disdain and lack of interest about their return or should I make a big fuss to give the impression that I missed them in some way? These situations must be so much easier for a dog — any fool can get excited and wag their tail. I'll just have to settle on the strategy that gets me the best outcome in terms of treats, tuna and attention.

Decisions, decisions…

AUGUST 19

Dear diary,

I've written in the past about the
village people (not the odd-looking
bunch who sang YMCA) and how
they are rather a mixed bunch,
with some that I really do not like.
However, there is one dear lady who
is a complete ray of sunshine and
brings goodness to cats who routinely
struggle to get the attention they
deserve. I call her Mrs Sunshine as when
she passes by she brings sunshine into my
life. She always has time to stop and dispense
some fuss: she's particularly good at tickling a cat
under its chin. That really does it for me and, and as an absolute
bonus, she always has a bag of cat treats in her pocket. If only
some other humans were as angelic as Mrs Sunshine.

She's the village's equivalent of Florence Nightingale, dispensing
love and care to the needy. I feel quite emotional just thinking
about her.

AUGUST 25

Dear diary,

It is just too hot.

The weather lady last night said it was going to reach 35 degrees and she was right.

Just remember, I wear a fur coat all year round and this temperature has gone beyond a joke. Even my eye balls are sweating.

AUGUST 28

Dear diary,

I need tuna.

I must have tuna.

But I feel like an astronaut cut adrift in space where no one can hear you scream. How do I make myself heard?

You don't need to take a spear down to the sea to try and catch one. Tuna comes conveniently packaged in tins in the supermarket. So why is it so difficult for humans to remember to buy me this good source of essential amino acids. Every week when he comes home from the supermarket, I wait in hope only to be disappointed again. Strangely, he manages to remember chocolate digestives and beer every week, but not tuna. I am crushed.

SEPTEMBER 4

Dear diary,

A little while back, following the crushing comments from the vet, I decided to go on a diet. Well, diary, I have tried. I've tried to cut down on the takeaways, and only have one or two a week. I had got into a bad routine of having a mouse most nights. I've not done too well on that aim, though I do question if there really is that much fat on a mouse. In fact, it would be most helpful if mice had those labels that you see on food packaging that show how many grams of fat and how much salt it contains.

The good news is that cutting down on cat treats has not been that difficult for me as the miserable humans have cut the supply off almost completely.

SEPTEMBER 7

Dear diary,

I think I have seen my first chav. I was snoozing in the sunshine on the top of the wall, when I heard this loud thumping noise that seemed to be getting nearer. Well, I thought it must be a tank or at least a steamroller, so imagine my surprise when the source of this noise appeared around the corner.

It was a Vauxhall Nova! At the wheel was a spotty youth and his music device, probably worth more than the car, was set to maximum and was delivering a thump, thump noise which he may have considered music but I considered to be a mobile migraine. As it went past, the thumping was so pronounced that it very nearly bounced me off the wall! I also noticed that he was wearing his baseball cap the wrong way round. I guess that's because his brain is in back to front.

SEPTEMBER 8

Dear diary,

Seems I'm not the only one who noticed the chav. The mobile thumping machine also caught the attention of Old Bert, who was, as is so often the case, fiddling with his marrows at the time. With impressive agility for an old git, he jumped out into the road in time to wave his fist at Mr Chav. As the Nova continued its thumping progress, the driver's peripheral awareness obviously permanently compromised by having bleeding ears, Old Bert was jumping up and down in the middle of the road, waving his garden fork. It sounded like he was shouting: "Noisy bugger eh, cowabunga! Nana Mouskouri, I'll 'ave 'ee on the way back Led Zeppelin, turnips!"

That's it, Bert. You tell him!

SEPTEMBER 13

Dear diary,

I'm working on my inner calm. I've realised that there have been rather too many points of tension and drama in my recent life and I need to focus on mindfulness. Being a cat brings many challenges and difficulties, but I am seeking a new, more simple and honest existence.

Please bring me some milk and tuna and then leave me alone. Thank you.

SEPTEMBER 14

Dear diary,

Well, my desire for mindfulness didn't last very long. Today, of all days, they've decided to redecorate the lounge and I know this will lead to upheaval, turmoil, disagreement and shouting. How can I work on my mindfulness in such a state of chaos? I'm thinking about offering myself up for rehoming but I'm worried that a new home might be even worse. Could that even be possible?

I may have to take my mindfulness into the garden. I hope it's not raining. Has anyone got any crystals?

SEPTEMBER 15

Dear diary,

I'm sad to report that my quest for mindfulness and an emotional sanctuary in the garden lasted about five minutes. I'd just found a quiet corner and was preparing to embark upon an intense session of meditation, which may have involved snoozing, when bloody Wodga decided to start mowing his lawn. He must have the noisiest lawnmower in Christendom and I reckon it can be heard in the next village. It probably interferes with air traffic control systems. Added to the noise, it seems to be powered by a 1970s diesel engine as his progress around his front garden is accompanied by acrid clouds of smoke.

In the words of Jim Royle: "Mindfulness, my arse!"

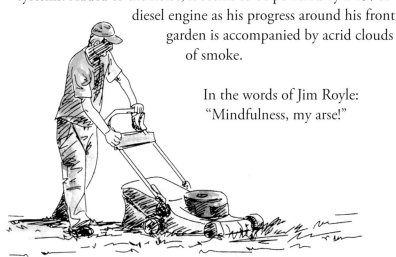

SEPTEMBER 16

Dear diary,

I think I might have scored a massive victory over Wodga and his ground-shaking lawnmower. As soon as I'd abandoned all hope of a mindfulness session in the garden, the leviathan coughed and stopped. Out of fuel it seemed, as I spied Wodga putting a jerry can in the back of his car and heading off to the garage for more diesel.

In a flash of inspiration, it all became clear to me. I hopped up onto the mower and to my great good fortune, he'd left the cap off the fuel tank. Being careful not to burn my nether regions on anything hot, I hoisted myself up and took a pee into the tank. It seemed to work perfectly, because upon his return I could hear Wodga cursing and kicking the mower when it stubbornly refused to restart. Powered by cat piss!

SEPTEMBER 19

Dear diary,

I want to discuss the role of the cat in popular culture. Honestly, I feel that we are being rather let down by the system. Sure, Dick Whittington's cat and Mr Mistoffelees have their place, but they're not very current, are they? Even my hero Garfield is showing his age a bit. And yet popular culture is full of dogs. One man and his dog, Lassie, K9, Turner and Hooch and countless epic journey home films have dogs cast in the lead role.

How about letting a cat solve a murder or two in Midsomer Murders'? We know more than we get credit for. Or how about "I'm a Cat, Get Me Out Of Here", "The Cat Factor", "Britain's Got Cats" or "The Only Way Is Moggie"? Frankly, I feel poorly represented in modern society.

SEPTEMBER 27

Dear diary,

I just don't get dogs. I was over
near the playing field earlier
today when one of the locals
turned up with their dog and
a tennis ball. The dog must have pretty modest life ambitions as
it seemed terribly excited about the whole deal. So, the human
throws the ball all the way across the field and the dog goes
running off after it, catches the ball and dashes back to its owner
and drops the ball at her feet. Then the whole charade was repeated
and this went on for some time!

I was aghast. I wouldn't have run off to get it the first time she
threw it away and most definitely would not have kept doing it
time after time. What an utterly pointless activity. If she wants
to throw the ball away, then let her. I'd have lost interest and
wandered off the first time she threw it.

Dogs: what are they like?

OCTOBER 2

Dear diary,

I need to explain one of the little injustices that I have to
deal with on an almost daily basis. When the humans have
a takeaway, they go to bed and leave the place looking like
a bomb site. Chinese food trays with the dregs of sweet and
sour chicken, or fish and chip wrappers or pizza boxes are left
all over the place. Do I complain? No, after a quick check to
see if anything edible has been left, I pick my way around the
detritus with good grace. But Lord help me if I dare to leave
any element of my takeaway on the floor: I get shouted at in no
uncertain terms. Usually, all I leave behind is the head of the
mouse and that internal organ which
always smells a bit funny.
It's nothing like the mess
they leave, but I always
get it in the neck.

It's not fair.

OCTOBER 6

Dear diary,

Good old Wodga the Wobba has been at it again. Earlier on,
I was out and about on a mid-morning patrol when two big vans
pulled up outside his house. Neither of them looked like Tesco or
Currys, so maybe they were not delivering. These four burly chaps
clambered out and started banging on Wodga's front door.

Interesting, I thought, as I settled down among the flowering heathers.

Well, Wodga duly opened the door and the whole thing very
quickly descended into a row with some rather choice language
used on both sides. After a bit of jostling, the chaps went inside
and soon re-emerged with the widescreen TV and the microwave.
Back in their vans they went and roared off, with Wodga running
up the road shouting about not being able to watch "Celebrity
Love Island"! Seems like the repo men have caught up with
naughty Wodga. It was all most enjoyable.

When Mrs Wodga wakes from her booze-induced slumber and
discovers that her two favourite domestic appliances are gone,
there's going to be a scene.

OCTOBER 8

Dear diary,

It is surely one of the great love stories of our time. Well, of our road, anyway. I refer, of course, to Trevor and his chickens. Scientists are sceptical that a chicken can reciprocate the love bestowed on it by a human but I'm going to beg to differ on that one. I was heading home the other morning as dawn was breaking and there was Trevor, checking on his girls and talking to them in hushed and rather emotional terms. I guess there is an uncomplicated relationship between a man and a chicken. As opposed to Trevor's relationship with Mrs Trevor, which seems to be based on fear, intimidation and a curious fetish for ornamental ironwork.

Poor, poor Trevor.

OCTOBER 14

Dear diary,

Celebrity.

Diary, this is a topic I shall come back to on a regular basis as I'm fascinated and bemused by it in equal measure and the tellybox on a Saturday night has a lot to answer for. The latest farrago involves some largely unknown but so-called celebrities trying their hands (and feet and legs) at ballroom dancing. It is essential viewing in the house, according to she who shall be obeyed. Why not just let the people who know how to do it get on with it? It's a bit like

letting me have a go at tig welding. I'd probably be a bit crap. Anyway, each of the celebs is paired with someone who can dance and, to me, the whole thing seems to be a competition to see how well a professional dancer can drag a sack of potatoes around the dance floor.

And they call it entertainment…

OCTOBER 21

Dear diary,

It has rained all day. My fur got soaked when
I dashed out to go to the toilet. I don't like
it. I shall spend the rest of the day snoozing,
grooming, dreaming of sunshine and, subject
to the ever-erratic human input, grazing.

Please do not disturb.

OCTOBER 24

Dear diary,

Is there a feline version of Childline? I wish there were because I'd have it on speed dial. My biggest single complaint is the radio. The humans seem to think it will be company for me if they leave it on all day when they go off to work. They really do not get it do they? My main activity while they are out is to sleep. How will wall-to-wall noise and irritating babble help me sleep? And have they listened to daytime radio? The pickings are slim to say the least. Commercial radio is a few songs interspersed by incredibly annoying adverts for carpets and plastic surgery and I'm not in the market for either of them.

And don't get me started on Radio 2…

Please, just turn it off when you leave the house!

NOVEMBER 1

Dear diary,

I do not like being laughed at. I'm not sure why it causes us cats so much angst, but if I get laughed at by humans I am prone to lose the plot. Last night was a case in point. The fire was on in the lounge, some mindless programme was on the tellybox and everyone seemed settled for the evening. Time, I thought, for some attention. So I hopped up onto her lap and did a few circuits before settling down for an evening snooze.

Everything was going well until she let out this enormous fart. In my sleep-muddled state, it took me completely by surprise and I accidentally rolled off onto the floor in an inelegant heap. I can't be sure if the ensuing roars of laughter were due to the fart or my plummet to the carpet; probably both. But I don't like being laughed at so I just had to make a run for it and leave the room at high speed. I duly found a quiet secluded corner to calm down and regain some of my dignity.

NOVEMBER 5

Dear diary,

I knew it was coming and it has arrived. Bonfire Night: one of my least favourite nights of the whole year. As you may imagine, I am of a rather nervous disposition and the whole evening leaves me traumatised and scared to go out. It has got nothing to do with fireworks: I'm quite partial to watching a few rockets heading into the sky. The bit that disturbs me is all those humans standing there and going ooooh and ahhhh all the time. For Christ sake, it is bonfire night. Why are you so surprised at the sight of fireworks? This year, the only redeeming moment was when one of the rockets misfired, shot off over the road and straight through the roof of Old Bert's shed...

Proper made my evening, it did.

NOVEMBER 7

Dear diary,

I've got sore feet.

Last night, I hopped up onto Wodga's shed for a night-time warm and, my god, it was even hotter than usual.

I hopped around a bit and had to bail out as my pads were being scorched. Talk about a cat on a hot tin roof! I guess he's turned up the heat as part of the harvesting process.

I wish someone had warned me but I guess there was a clue in the fact that the three extension cables running from the house to the shed were so hot that they were making the wet grass steam.

NOVEMBER 12

Dear diary,

Children's television is an instrument of torture.

Thankfully, our two have now grown up a bit and spend most of their time peering at their ipads. But I still remember the trauma of children's TV programmes blaring out when I was trying to sleep.

Does anyone remember "In the Night Garden"? It was truly disturbing with characters like Iggle Piggle, Upsy Daisy and Makka Pakka. Apparently, it was meant to prepare children for sleep but all it did for me was induce nightmares.

I think the people who produced it might have been using too much of Wodga's herbal remedy! There were other unhinged programmes around at the same time, but this one really took the biscuit.

NOVEMBER 14

Dear diary,

I hear that risk assessments are the in thing right now.

Before you do anything, you should assess the risk of being injured or worse. On that basis, I think Trevor should do a risk assessment before going within 20 feet of Mrs Trevor. However, it strikes me that more people die in bed than anywhere else, so surely going to bed is the riskiest thing a human can do. I reckon they should leave their beds to us cats and spend the night on a kitchen chair. After all, when was the last time you heard of someone dying on a kitchen chair?

NOVEMBER 15

Dear diary,

To continue on the theme of risk assessments…
I decided to do a risk assessment before leaving the house.

Risk of being soaked by Old Bert — high.
Risk of being chased out of the garden by Wodga — high.
Risk of being mooned by Ginge — high.
Risk of encountering Mrs Trevor — high.

Oh dear, I've just realised what a cruel and dangerous place the world really is. I'm going back to bed.

NOVEMBER 22

Dear diary,

Oh joy of joys. Can a cat be any more happy?

It is late November and he has finally relented and put the log fire on in the lounge. After several weeks of her concerted grumbling and whinging, he finally caved in and lit the fire. Of course, we had all his annual moans: logs don't grow on trees, you know; it's like a sauna in here; it's so hot my eyeballs are drying out and so on. But I don't care because stretched out in front of a log fire is one of my truly happy places. I hope it will now become a regular feature of the next few months.

NOVEMBER 26

Dear diary,

Nothing at all happened today.

Nothing.
Zero.
Zilch.

That is all I have to say on the matter of international nothing day.

DECEMBER 3

Dear diary,

I can feel a rant coming on. Last night, the family was sat staring at the tellybox and I was only half-paying attention when a thing came on about celebrities doing weird stuff. I can't really remember if they were supposed to be eating kangaroo testicles or snogging each other by the pool; it's probably difficult for humans to tell the difference. Anyway, what struck me, as I pretended to doze by putting on a mid-level purr, was the use of the term celebrity. Now call me old-fashioned if you will, but I thought a celebrity was someone who had done something pretty special or was good at things like telling jokes or singing. Well, this bunch of people I'd never heard of didn't seem to have any discernible talent, other than an apparent willingness to eat kangaroo testicles. In fact, some of them were most definitely swimming in the shallow end of the gene pool. Very odd.

DECEMBER 7

Dear diary,

Today was a nice day, just enjoying the simple things in life.

I had some breakfast, had a snooze, went for a little potter outside, had a poo, came back in, slept some more, had my tea and then had a snooze on his lap in front of the tellybox. I didn't get into trouble, no one shouted at me and I even felt a bit loved.

Just a nice day.

That probably means that it will all turn to shit tomorrow!

DECEMBER 12

Well, what excitement! The gales last night blew a rather large tree
down across our road and the way to the outside world was cut-off
this morning. As soon as our predicament became apparent, all
the neighbours gathered together to try and come up with a plan
to effect our escape. This should be a laugh, I thought, as I settled
down to watch developments: it was like a scene from a disaster
movie and I half-expected Harrison Ford to appear with a gun and
a coiled rope. Well, first to offer his view was The Snowflake who
wanted to send a strongly-worded letter to the local Highways
Authority about tree safety. Barely had they finished shouting
him down when Nervous Nellie appeared on the other side of the
tree. Once she'd realised the situation, she turned on her heels and
legged it, wringing her hands together. Mr Beige Honda Jazz man
made a valuable contribution by revealing that it
was an ash tree and kept everyone amused
with interesting facts about the ash.

To be continued…

DECEMBER 13

Dear diary,

The fallen tree part two: next to take centre stage was
Wodga, who said he could get a good deal for the firewood.
Well done, Wodga, always looking for a chance to make a pound.
Trevor the chicken whisperer stood to one side, not saying much
and then periodically leant over his garden wall to reassure his
chickens that everything would be alright. Then, the intellectual
heavyweight, Old Bert, weighed in and said something that
sounded like: "Gert big ash, ah windy night and turnip!
I knowed it and told that Mrs Higginbottom that they roots
were all durdled." The situation seemed hopeless but then, from
round the back of Trevor's house came the unmistakable roar
of a chainsaw being started. Sure enough, Mrs Trevor appeared,
swathed in two-stroke smoke, wearing big leather gauntlets,
a woodman's safety helmet and visor and swinging a chain saw like
Mick Jagger with a guitar, or even a scene from the Texas Chainsaw
Massacre. It was inspirational and terrifying
in equal measure, but Mrs Trevor made
short work of the tree and the road
was soon open again. She truly is a
formidable woman!

DECEMBER 18

Dear diary,

I reckon good old Wodga the Wobba has joined the Freemasons or some other secret organisation. Late last night I was out and about when a car pulled up outside his gates and the driver started flashing the headlights like he was spelling out some sort of code. Wodga appeared pretty smartish carrying a couple of packages, opened his garden gates and handed the packages through the back window of the car, which opened just low enough. I couldn't see who was in the back of the car as it had those darkened windows. All very curious. But on balance, I suspect it was rather dodgy. Of course, they might have been collecting old shoes to send to the under-privileged in a third world country, but it was odd to be doing charity work so late at night…

DECEMBER 25

Dear diary,

It must be Christmas again. The kids were up and tearing around the house at some ungodly hour and there is now wrapping paper all over the floor of the lounge. But it seems that, as usual, I've been completely ignored. How difficult can it be to wrap up some cat treats and a tin of tuna for goodness sake? Clearly Santa didn't get my letter so I'll have to resort to plan B and hang around the kitchen hoping for a bit of roast turkey. Seems like it is the season of goodwill to all men, but not to cats. Bah humbug!

DECEMBER 26

Dear diary,

Christmas Day part 2.

Well, the festive occasion fully lived up to my low expectations.
There were, indeed, no presents for me whatsoever. Everyone else
got hideous jumpers, nasty smelling perfume and sundry other tut,
but absolutely nothing for surely the most popular member of the
family. It got worse later on when Aunty Doris arrived for lunch.
She claims to be a cat lover, but always manages to put me through
the terrible ordeal of being picked up and kissed. Her overload of
perfume is enough to make a cat puke. In fact, I did think about
sicking up a fur ball just to show my true feelings.

Thankfully, by late afternoon most of the adults were comatose
in the lounge, pretending to watch the King's speech.

DECEMBER 28

Dear diary,

Christmas is surely the time for festive cheer, eating too much and watching old films. Well last night, they put on a film called "The Shining". It sounded quite an upbeat title to me, so I was half watching it while having a good grooming session on his lap. But dear God, why did no one warn me about the bathroom scene when Jack Nicholson sticks his head through the door and says: "Here's Johnny!"

It scared the bejesus out of me and I very nearly made a bit of a mess in his lap. Why couldn't they have watched "Tootsie" or "When Harry met Sally"?

I'm still trembling.

DECEMBER 31

Dear diary,

Well, we have come to the end of the year and it is a time to reflect on the highs and lows of my feline existence.

There has been drama, excitement, sleep, danger, abject boredom, sleep, comfort, discomfort, fear, sleep and mad humans but not enough tuna.

Trevor has survived another year of terror-based wedlock, Old Bert has become an even bigger scrote, Wodga has sailed close to the wind and Mrs Wodga has done wonderful charity work with her support for the local off-licence.

My humans have muddled through another year without doing themselves serious harm and that yappy dog next door has lived longer than I had planned.

Overall, score seven out of ten, could do better.

See you next year!